WALRUS NEEDS A HOME

Written by:
A V Owen

Illustrations:
Maria F. Rojas

ISBN:
978-989-33-1401-2

www.anasfables.com

To my amazing, kind, creative, clever, resilient, empathetic, caring, loving and hilarious sons, Isaac and Oscar. You will both always be my inspiration.

The migration of Wesley Walrus
with his children Wendy and Will,

Was when the proud father told of generations
who found their home most brill.

Finally, the three at their new home arrived,
Wesley Walrus to his beloved children advised.

Then all of a sudden a worried Wendy wined, "Daaaad..."
To which Will Walrus added,

Daaaaaad...

Just look behind you.
You best had.

Wesley Walrus was shocked to see the beach
he remembered with plenty of space,
The beach he thought would provide his family's perfect base,

Was now full to the brim, he exclaimed:

What a disgrace. For years walruses have been coming to this place.

Looking at the worried expressions on the faces of Wendy and Will. Wesley Walrus announced:

Through the sleeping walruses quietly
not to wake them, they go.

Jumping, squeezing and squishing
the dozing walruses below.

The three finally reached the end of the beach,
Ahead of them was an enormous cliff,
the top they wanted to reach.

Climbing is awfully difficult for
a walrus, as you know.

The higher they climbed there
was less and less snow.

Finally, the three at their new home arrived,
Wesley Walrus to his beloved children advised.

Wendy, Will...
just look at that view!

I told you the climb
would be worth it.
I did. I told you!

Then all of a sudden a worried Wendy wined, "Daaaad…"
To which Will Walrus added

Wesley Walrus was shocked to see the cliff
he remembered with plenty of space,
The cliff he thought would provide his family's perfect base,
Was now full to the brim, he exclaimed:

Looking at the worried expressions on the faces of Wendy and Will. Wesley Walrus announced:

Through the sleeping walruses
quietly not to wake them, they go.

Jumping, squeezing and squishing
the dozing walruses below.

The three finally reached the edge of the cliff,
As they looked down the sense of danger was swift.

For the first time the children saw their father sad.
Wendy brokenheartedly sighed, "Oh Dad"

Will Walrus took action and said:

Let's go find our new home!

His children's hope filled Wesley Walrus's heart,
which encouraged him to continue his roam.

Together they slid down
the dangerous cliff,
through the packed beach
and into the cold sea.

Where they jumped on board an ice plate
just big enough for three.

Until this day Wesley Walrus remains confused at
what could have changed, the size of the land
where his ancestors used to happily be.

But this was now the very same land
that the three had to flee.

WESLEY, WILL AND WENDY
A beautiful Walrus family!

Did you know?

With their long tusks, loveable whiskers and their enormous size there is no confusing the walrus with any other animal on Earth.

A walrus

A Human and a Car

Lifestyle

Walruses are very sociable animals and so enjoy living in groups. The largest group ever recorded was of approximately 5,000 walruses.

A group of walruses is called a herd and In the wild walruses can live up to 40 years of age.

THEY'RE SO BIG!!

How Many?

It is estimated that the number of walruses in the wild is in the region of 250,000.

LET US SLEEP PLEASE!

CAN YOU IMAGINE 250.000 WESLEYS? PARADISE!!!

So Chilly!

Due to the layers of blubber underneath their skin, walruses can survive in very cold climates. They are also able to slow down their heart rate to be able to live comfortably in the Arctic. Walruses can live in temperatures as low as -35 ºC. **Now that is cold!**

Yummy!

Walruses love to munch down on clams, octopus, prawns and sea cucumbers. Sometimes they also hunt fish such as the polar cod. Walruses can dive up to 90 metres into the ocean to look for food.

I'M NOT EVEN COLD!

Climate Change

The effects of global warming are having a devastating effect on the Arctic. The rising temperatures mean that the Antarctica ice sheets and sea ice is melting.

This means that with every passing year there is less space for walruses like Wesley, Will and Wendy to safely live, feed and breed on shore. In 2019 more than 500 walruses died due to the effect of Climate Change on their habitat.

HELP!

LET'S TALK WITH AN EXPERT!
Laura Jourdan!

SHE'S AMAZING!

"*What I like the most about walruses is their social interactions. They are very social animals and watching them interacting is amazing, interesting and sometimes hilarious.*

I particularly love the very close bond between the mother and the calf, even though I have never experienced it visually. But I know that the cows take care of their calf for at least two years, which is a record in the pinniped's kingdom.

Laura Jourdan is a Biologist, Polar Expedition Guide and wildlife photographer. She has led 6 expeditions to Antarctica and 6 to the Arctic. Laura has seen many walruses in their natural environment. Laura does this in the hope to raise awareness and to promote conservation efforts. Laura recalls:

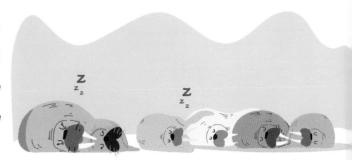

Most of the other seal species nurse their pup for a couple of weeks only. I also love the fact that such huge animals actually eat mainly clams! They need to eat as many as 400 of them every day to survive! To find the clams, they survey the ocean's floor with their very sensitive whiskers, sweep the sand off the clams with their pectoral fins, then place their lips on each side of the shell and create a vacuum in their mouth to suck the mollusk out of its shell.
They actually have the strongest suction force in the animal kingdom!"

During this time Laura has noticed a real change in the sea ice, as well as the pluri. The pluri-annuelle is the ice that doesn't melt in summer. Every year there is less and less. Laura says that, *"This is a very alarming situation for all the wildlife that depends on it to rest, to feed and to breed, including the walruses."*

If you would like to see more of Laura's beautiful photographs, learn more about her adventures or even go on an adventures with her you can find everything you need to know on her website, **www.laurajourdan.com**

Printed in Great Britain
by Amazon

56007153R00024